BATHERS

ALSO BY

ROBERT STEINER

Quill (novel)

ROBERT STEINER

BATHERS

A
NEW DIRECTIONS
BOOK

IN MEMORIAM

Judith Maxwell

1943–1977

The author gratefully acknowledges the financial assistance of the National Endowment for the Arts in the writing of this book.

Portions of this book have appeared, in different versions, in *Canto*, *Itinerary*, and *New Directions in Prose and Poetry 34*.

Manufactured in the United States of America
First published in 1980 in a limited edition, signed by the author and printed at The Stinehour Press, Lunenburg, Vermont, and as New Directions Paperbook 495
Published simultaneously in Canada by George J. McLeod Ltd., Toronto

LIBRARY OF CONGRESS CATALOGING IN PUBLICATION DATA
Steiner, Robert, 1948–
Bathers.
(A New Directions Book)
I. Title.
PZ4.S823Bat 1979 [PS3569.T376] 813'.5'4 79-23084
ISBN 0-8112-0752-8
ISBN 0-8112-0753-6 pbk.

Designed by Roderick Stinehour

New Directions Books are published for James Laughlin
by New Directions Publishing Corporation,
80 Eighth Avenue, New York 10011

I

I AM FAMILIAR with the movement of the flatworm and the bee. I know what it is the snail sees in its shell. I, who have measured life among brittle petals, am soothed only by the delicate motor of a grasshopper's legs. Catching a wasp by its wings in the fury of its passage is an art I have known since childhood.

I know that if you boil the lotus in water you create the finest perfume in history: sprinkle your naked parts with lotus water before going to the summer outdoors and bees will not sting you but only come to suck: toads are fearsome and devour the larvae that grasp your tender ferns: the cava weed, which sits in the garden like a lynx at the foot of a queen, emanates an amphor of lotus. These are matters of substance. These are natural properties.

Call it quest or theft, it is the nostalgia for perfection. The hunt for a magical skin. The Christmas cactus requires twelve hours each day of uninterrupted blackness in order to flower. The bark of the banana will provide the softest sole for your shoes. I possess the knowledge that will save you yanking weeds week after week before guests arrive for croquet and gin rickeys.

Citizen: the sun-dried matter: a bone found on the beach: the rune cut into stone. I have the form for perfection. I can project it: why there are Gauchos in the pampas, movie stars in new wallets, why presidents and priests: why blind Marius is our potter.

Our women do not collaborate horizontally with aliens. We cook fish in the milk of an ass. In our myth we are born of the swallowed brain of a magpie: once, we were two-headed and ripped the hearts of enemies with the talons that were our hands. We pray for the death of the reticulate snake. Our eternity is constructed: from the tawny throats of women dangle amulets with stars: our women speak nonsense to the sick so that the sick die glimpsing eternal unreality. Marius the blind potter has told us how the toad loved the tarantula beside the road. For us an eye is a balcony: the sea is a net: like the bird we know that if it were not for air we would be free.

In the yellow moist eyes of horses my people see themselves. On the broken backs of donkeys their defeat travels. Brace of rabbits in a torn sack: wooden black madonnas carved for sale: fleas, lice, the horse that pisses near their pillows. We undo history. Our myth has an ictus. Imagine the beehives, citizen, which bask like pineapples in the lattice of my rooftop. All colors and songs of bird eat from our sea. A fleet of vessels waits with foreign flags: the walls of our cafés are riddled by bullet holes: warplanes swoop like gun metal out of the sun: that is what I want you to imagine. And the sight outside my villa of fierce ants descending from a hot sand hill to a drying sumptuous fig.

When the time came I too would remember how fungus ravaged my leaves, how a glotty sap broke the tender skin of roots. Nut grass flourished like hair. I would remember that I rolled breathlessly from under bedsheets to torch a fire stark in the night as tiger eyes. Magnifier in one trembling hand, flashlight in the other I would journey barefoot to the garden which divided my shocking white villa from the intruding woods. The coarse iris of a rose stared pale and clotted toward the potting shed door. Threads of smoke rose from my garden.

Through the uniform rows I stalked crouched and relentless, toes curling into the soil from the chill. I heard creatures baying in the mountain, frightened predators in rocky shafts of brush, of lichen. I would light then the fire, as if it were a signal to the camps in the mountain. I would sit so long in the middle of the night that I would forget why I had come out. Ponchita could be seen stirring from bed, tossing aside a gown or stepping into the legs of underpants.

I was seed juggler, tender of the lotus and the rose. I would examine in my Congolese fatigues the gargoyle faces and muffin-gray petals that resembled tears on sleeping eyelids. By neither night nor day, sunlight nor incendiary fire could I save my hybrids. I wrapped them in gauze. I treated them with antiseptics. Before long, before I crushed between my palms the first moth of spring I had impacted my hybrids in dangerous powders. Soon I was splicing roots and grafting, and then, at last, uprooting with the grim determination of an abortionist. Did Ponchita understand? Did she recognize my will and ferocity?

With my apprentice Rudy I would protect the barbarous plants and ignore completely the richness, the delicacy of my hybrids. I cultivated weeds about my dows, I gave spiny hideous creations the hard hours of morning and the mulch of vitamins born at the bottom of my mortar and relinquished from my palm. I watched Rudy polish his muscles in the heat of the garden. I looked fearfully at my sunning Ponchita. Over coffee fallen cold during my lament to her she utterly and sincerely agreed. I grieved. We had to let the hybrids go.

You must imagine now the high roll of the sea when a

cruising vessel or great foreign liner approaches: the intrepid lemon nature of the village as the sun creeps above the promontory that slices the sea: crowds bathing below the calm sweep of loons with small fish in the hollows of their bills: the awkwardness of flushed tourists drinking granitas in the weak shade of an awning: bored women in mushroom hats of straw holding my palm in the hottest part of the day only to feel it dry and stiff as a shell on the beach. The smell of sailors, of dreamy young widows who cannot stand the feel of animal skin against them. They come wearing artificial rubies on their toes: they sink easels the length of a leg into the beach: rocks, like sleeping lizards, are stools for their feet. Passing burnt faces and postures rumpled by the effort of rising again to their feet I balance a lean leggy spider on the knuckle of one hand. A vital young girl pretends for a moment she is loose and alone, leans a hip against a wall and draws up one knee so that the curve of her thigh faces the Arab alley. And sporting a beyedere scarf at her throat an ugly woman waits for a friend while drinking lemon squash through a straw.

May the browser beware. Do not enter the cinnamon smell and olive haze of our village without the obscurity of passion. Those who are hopeless arrive protected: those in love come adorned: those whose hearts have shredded with disease find their minds eager to follow. The sturdy nature of our piscators and our buxom sweaty women serves only to make the weak weaker, the suffering suffer more. Our men are fat as rabbits; our women bloat with fever from giving birth—they squat in olive groves, in lime orchards, they drop babies into scarves. Foreigners are faced with the nightmare of what they cannot become. Steamers bring foreigners hoping to grow experience as if it were hair.

—Is there anything like a Pan-American highway? You people can't seem to make a road.

—Nobody twisted my arm. I like it here. I didn't say I didn't like it. I'm having a wonderful time so shut up.

—You don't mean to say there is only *gazate* to drink?

—Don't badger the people. I don't like being cheated any more than you. Yet they are courteous.

—You don't happen to have any poisonous or flesh-eating plants, do you? It's for my wife.

I am at my best, citizen, when it is time to do business. The coming of a scorcher, a ninety-degree dawn, tourists lusting for a foreign taste. Their coins are of wondrous shape, texture, and smell. In my white linen suit I deal not as a tradesman but as a stranger conspiring with a patron to explain beauty. Their cameras shoot me. Their hands hold my flowers as if they are eggs, as if they are a baby's testicles. I know from their pimento eyes and smiles that they are seasick, overfed, sun-drugged. They have begun to believe that their homes are being looted in their absence.

—What caused all this? I am often asked.

This is where I live.

—Centuries of weather and misery.

—I see, and they meditate.

There are the tired anointing each other with ointments against heat, sun, disease, and sin. They appear like a flock of geese, craning, feathered, white into their souls. They burst from doorways; we watch them from above, standing at dark open windows. Laughing, lifting sunglasses, women in summer skirts wave to us their tall rum or sherry drinks in cups of fluted wood.

I serve them all. I am their servant under the perpetually awesome sky, only a few steps from the fountain where lovers invest their smallest coin in magic, from the cathedral whose doors boom and whose spires provide shade. In the aura of our dead lava promontory and white village the tourists study every facet of my trade, of me, the industry of my personal style, and see through it all a theory I bring. I am the reason they have come, or at least that is what they will tell themselves when they are safely home. They do not trust my judgment or my person; I sympathize with their mistrust.

—I have what you want, I say modestly.

When I speak up it is not the flatus of ambition. They sample my flowered kiosk. They are only tuning their senses though they do not know it at the time. I show bunches, sprigs and sprays in white and yellow tissue. I show three sizes of pottery buffed smooth and aromatic. It is then that I tell them of nosegays, wristlets, garlands, a wreath. Nothing of course can be quite so exotic as the single perfect lotus or rose. I touch madame's sculptured bun, I indicate her bosom. I offer them one, only one, waiting in a humidor moist, fragrant, cool, cut and naturally tubed. One is a tender umbrella, petals firm but full and bent as a goat's ear. A natural silence follows because of the price. Patience is my investment; theirs is only money. They wish to believe they have been cheated by someone of distinction, or they wish to patronize a man of craft. The buttonhole is filled, the hand grasps, the wrist poises. Desperate people guard their flower. They see to it other travelers smell it too. It will be carried and pressed, and it will remind them of me, of us, where they were last summer, what they thought they could be, what they are and have and want. The rose, the lotus, are not postcards. They are not slides, skirts, nor even rugs or hats. They are the brief sensation. They carry their decay in their beauty and are the weariness of the traveler's body. They are for the imagination.

I would remember all these things, citizen. I would see them as familiar ghosts. As translucent and sculptured as my last look at the shadow of Rudy roaring down the steep dusty slope and rapidly changing the gears on his motorbike. The broad cycle belt, the bitterness of his high ratty hair, the include-me-out expression of his jackboots on the silver pedals. His was the desperate flourish of the traveler. I would remember his looking for an object.

Had I not left them sunning naked while I searched the woods for honeycombs? Did I not in fact wear Congolese fatigues when I spread myself near them? He buttered her legs: she polished his chest: together they drew our variety of screaming brown flies. They ate figs while I cracked nuts between thumb and forefinger. Did they not swim raw and dark beyond the breakers, though I waded not ten feet from shore with our dog? They would drink in dance music at night. I heard the terrible news in our broad-hipped toothy radio. I would wrestle the dog, they observing with cool glorias in their hands. And at last, Ponchita said, I must have known what was approaching, only a tree could be so blind.

Rudy, as I could see his muscular adoloscent shadow, tapped his fingernails on our bedroom door. His other hand quietly revolved the door knob as he listened with impatience and fear. I had watched them for weeks from the garden where I dug into the sodbed. I had watched them smirk from wooden chairs and nod with vexation at my energy, my compassion. They rolled their tongues over glassy cubes of ice and finally, with a feint of sadness, settled watery eyes on each other. I had pushed them to it, Ponchita said. She threw a Dutch wooden clog at me from across the room. Rudy continued to tap at the door above.

Suddenly Ponchita had vanished. Our staircase was vacant, the top of the steps and hall dark, empty, the bedroom door at last quietly crossed and shut with deliberation. I stood at the lung of our fireplace, hands thrust into the pockets, the deep wells of my fatigues. I would remember that our villa rested on trestles and that the wind made floors creak. Behind us a half mile into the mountain an abandoned tower was engulfed by banana and rubber trees: I could see the tower through binoculars, past the rough treetops: I could look toward the village from our roof and see the steeple and parapet of the cathedral, the Moorish spires above the cul-de-sac where our visitors pivot.

The scream of the wind silenced us, left us to feel mortal, like capitalists when they suffer our sunrise. The scream could force me to uncork yet another bottle of wine. Warped shelves of brick and knotty lumber leaned with preserves and plants in every room but the bath. There were traces of top-soil on each piece of furniture, a smell of humus in our clothes. A phonograph sat across from my radio, its tulip emitting the scratches to which Ponchita and Rudy danced.

They moved toward each other from a distance, each tempting the other to place the first hand. He would hover at her throat, milky thoughtless eyes following a vein of moisture that began in the cave of her chin and slid until it glowed above her breasts. They moved little. They stared unashamed and took no notice of me in the fat armchair beside the radio. Fingers holding my temples, a cracked warm headset jacked into the console and strapped about my head, I would lift one leather ear to follow the tempo. Their sweat would run in earnest then. Rudy planted his nose, sniffed and came away with a shine on his face. And last, when I fully raised my head from the horror of the word mongers, they would stand almost still, suspended, perfectly relaxed with their arms entangled like war-scarred friends reunited in a street. The volume was tipped high: weary eyes were lidded tight: the female fog of a voice went on and on with its *doovoo, doovoo, je vous*, that sort of song, a song for men trapped in bunkers. Suddenly the song would stop, the needle begin a rasp which it repeated and repeated until Rudy started the disc spinning again.

And yes, I had seen the blade of his tongue pierce her lips —it stole into the funnel of her mouth. They believed they were safe in the potting shed. Though privacy is awkward I could not expose theirs to any worse or less generous fate than simply to be observing the unsophisticated kiss.

Once, when they had gone together to the village but quickly returned, I saw them from the garden, saw Rudy toss her abruptly from the motorbike and soar into the mountain toward the camps.

—Shall we do a little weeding? I asked.

Ponchita went inside without answering. For a time I pulled rampant onions, until I heard the whistle and drumbeat of the plumbing and knew she was filling the bath. I stood against my hoe, kicked sod from my shoes with one foot, then the other, looking down the road and listening. I decapitated an onion. Because Rudy did not return I scrubbed my hands, used them to drive back the hair from my face and offered to soap her myself. A drop of water from the tap struck her foot steadily.

Is it not monstrous to fear every blemish on your body, each smell you have grown used to, simply because you are in the naked presence of your wife? Is there not something rueful in having to clear your throat and rub your eye, then stare at the finger you use to rub, while you are thinking of something to say? She submerged her breasts but they floated loyally to the surface, they swayed in the bursting suds. Ponchita smoked moons at me when I placed a cigar between her teeth and her lips closed thickly, serenely around the butt end. She accused me of moodiness. I fluttered my hand in the water, I teased her with fingers as she turned onto her stomach. We vegetated in silence for a humid minute, staring in opposite directions at different and yet the same white walls: folds in her kimono which hung on a hook, her sash mysteriously still in a bow. She tossed the cake of soap at her feet. She stopped me with a soapy foot raised against my chin.

I waited for a tremor in her lips, the birth of a tic at the pulse of her neck. Instead she rose, towering above me, dripping freely, her hair waxy and gnarled. She lifted her calf over the rim of the tub and her vagina yawned. I pedaled backward until with a toe polished fish-silver she cracked the door shut. We spoke through the louvers.

She said she could promise to be noisy with Rudy, to scream through the house the words and senseless sounds she knew I liked to hear. But I was forbidden to share their bed, could not even lie against the wall poised on my ribs only, an arm under my head, face to the window. I promised that I would not touch or asked to be touched.

—One emotional center, she said quietly.

I entered to remind her of something in her past. She would not talk to me again. With her figure exaggerated and inhuman as she felt for lumps in her breasts I turned shivering and shut her in behind me. So when Ponchita finally crept to my armchair I continued to poke last winter's ashes, to listen to the music in my chimney. My radio was buzzing, my headset crackled from a thunderstorm. I watched her kneel at my knees, place a hand on my belly: her knuckles were swollen, her hands crusty from the sun. Voices began to arrive through the static. The streets were crowding with thirsty babies in the arms of angry mothers, dugs dry, wombs growing again.

—Did you hear me? she said.

—And do you understand? she said.

She sighed, sat tired, squat-legged, hesitant before me. She tightened her kimono until her breasts archly informed the ferns of the design. She asked would I like an egg.

—You mean *an* egg?

—An *egg*.

—As from a chicken or goose? An egg in that sense?

—In the sense of a duck.

—Oh. A duck's egg then you mean.

—Duck's egg. Yes.

I lit a cigar. Again she sighed, this time yawning too, too tired to disguise the yawn, as if her yawning could mean anything more to me than that it was dark, the end of a strenuous exacting day, that Rudy was late. I knew of course how late it was: I had reached Cairo on the radio.

It was good, she said, spring had come early. The sea air would rorify the ground. Sheep, she assured me, would now be grazing handsomely. Goats. The flowers, Ponchita said tenderly, might no longer die. The rose. The lotus. She moved and the dishes of her knees seemed pale, bone white and flat, the shinbones glowing under her skin. I leaned toward her parting words.

—I know it will be hard for you. Terribly hard.

And yet, once Ponchita had bounded the stairs, once Rudy had managed to find room in my large bed space, after she had attacked me with her shoe, the images in my mind did not wander uselessly. The thunderheads clapped in the mountain: the heavy sky still allowed me to see the white sheet of moonlight cover our dead smoking whale. I sat in the kitchen thinking that I was yet in the room with them. In every puff and heave. My odor was in the wood, my shadow indented the sagging mattress: my collection of shards and island relics on shelves, dresser top, before mirrors staring them down to make my absence their burden: fifty rare bottles on the wardrobe floor: my jellaba of blue and yellow stripes draped across the chair at the window: my worm courge and the newts Miguel and Dave. They could not remove the lucid light of my eyes peering at them from every corner of hiding.

Yes, Ponchita's cheeks pucker and her eyes are orientally narrow. The palms of her hands are aged, and low along the furrow of her spine is a mole I nibble late into the night. Face hawklike, powdery, sand along her hairline: her feet wiry, toenails thick and grained like fresh pine: nipples like oysters, teeth yellow from the frequent cigar, tight knots of hair under her arms—Ponchita, sexing a stranger, a boy joined to our family, nuzzling, plying his blond jungle of hair, his lumps of untested strength and toughness. There was simply no deed they could perform I could not imagine: no body or butterfly kiss I had not given or received. They had no hope of intimacy, of the kind of trust or faith that Ponchita suggested. At the kitchen table I studied shreds of orange on Rudy's pocket knife and measured Ponchita's teeth marks in a wedge of hardening cheese. I wanted to warn them about Ponchita's scabbed heel.

I would remember the photograph, taken by Rudy, of my wife beside the motorbike. His machine oily and tendriled, with chrome and silver thorax, a leather groin with stars emblazoned on the tool bag. My tulips, a clump of thistle at her feet, Ponchita raised a dancer's foot as if about to touch a chilly stream. Behind her a smoky hill, sunset brewing through the clouds. Afterward she, Rudy, and I drank mint tea and ate sticky buns. I could see wrinkles in the countryside even then. Anxious, waiting even then, at old gay times, watching over Ponchita. Piscators knitted nets, a toe described the loop that kept the hemp taut: hungry goblin ladies wore dead foxes in the city at night: there were plenty of figs: it was there, not quick as the brilliance of a struck match, in the stewing lamb, the heavy smell of olive groves, the restlessness and cheer of a hundred mountain fires: there in the boggishness and ease, the heat and dust, more fear each day. During storms virgins suffered rape, blood suckers crept into the village in satin formals, dogs bayed along the avenue of the rich: Caid, at noon on the beach with his burro, frightened the tourists. Even then, cruel forces were at prey. I left a sweat mark, my thumbprint, on the photograph of Ponchita's red halter.

Daylight shattered. Night opened darker than a pocket. The silence was a conspiracy of desire. I had seen her bathe Rudy's back in our deep tub: they had napped on the pebbled beach with legs designed around each other like wrestlers, and when I awakened them there was no embarrassment: there had been no furtive acts, no secret touching of hands. As darkness opened a dark gate I sensed the fleshlessness of them as lovers. I experienced their desperation. I stood at the staircase hoping to hear them. Or I sat rubbing my feet on the tiles of the veranda. Or watching the dog's fast heart as he slept on my legs. The ache in the bones behind my ears was profounder even than the silence, a lumbering sea whose significance eluded me, as had the moment of Ponchita's resolution.

Uncovering the sinking sweltering condition, the tremors, riots, rapes, executions—my certitude had provoked her. Even as Ponchita might, by withdrawing to the impulsive world that Rudy knew, discover a new need, I would yet go forth to penetrate terror, the heart of my village, in the ruinous woods, by the violence of the radio. And suddenly, with images of plunder in my mind, Ponchita's grievous moans pierced the silence. The setter lifted an eyelid, glanced at the vacant stairs, then lapped at the hair of my shin. He sank down on my feet to hold me in his warm weight in the middle of the stark moony kitchen where I stood.

I listened. I wanted their night to continue. Could they say the same? Speaking to me, in a sense, they were honest, fearful, timid—therefore brash. Later, wearing my blue and yellow jellaba, a sleep-eyed Rudy came down for a cup of tea. I had been brewing it for some time. Out in the garden, upon a clutch of notorious ragweed, he urinated as I had asked. His lip was swollen with passion and he fingered it cautiously. I asked if he wanted to have tea in the bedroom—Ponchita, I explained, was fond of taking tea afterward, and I was prepared to make a tray. Rudy let his eyes wander. He scratched the dog's flanks with a toe, then sliced and bit the quarter of a mushy lemon. He said that in his dream he realized that he could achieve a greater sexual release than I would ever know. I replied that I never dream and that release I did not identify with sex. When Rudy asked for a bun I refused because it was not in the style of Ponchita's need. He took the tray of tea and lemon from my hands, took it to my wife and left the door ajar less than the width of a finger. Inside the lights remained dead. I could hear only the burbling of tea and the sucking of lemon.

Before dawn I stood on the veranda feeling the wet breeze invade the passages of my ears and nose. In the village white smoke rose where Marius the blind potter was firing his kiln. Our horizon of ruthlessness, of destruction crawled toward daylight when I began to hear from the far side of the mountain the hum of warplanes. A boat skulked to sea carrying fugitives in the dress of our piscators. Once the sky was light the warplanes would flash through a cloud, flush the boat out of the water with small missiles and disappear again behind the promontory. Heedless of village smoke, untuned to the vast box of voices, never having felt the tremor as I did, my wife and the apprentice could linger in their fantasy the way our chameleons sleep in the mimosa coiled by snakes.

I should have disturbed them. Instead I stepped back into the shadow of the roof below their window. I should have shared my experience. They ought to have come down. A star descending with a trail of blood into the sea: a meeting by its light in a dangerous alley café: a boat off shore that kept the motor running: flowers reaching like shrunken arms from buried bodies. The villa did not stir. I saw dogs sniffng for bombs that may have been attached to clocks—between rocks in the wash of our grotto, buried in castles of sand along the crowded beach, or placed like a lost shoe in some remote thicket. Hounds smelled our village, sailors' rank duffels, the leafy woods. Of course Ponchita and Rudy did not come down, could not. And when the time came I would recall that every day the skid marks of Ponchita's nails went deeper into Rudy's back. Each day long scabs formed over the wounds and were torn away at night. I would remember that unlike my own, Rudy's flesh was vulnerable.

I listened far into the spring, after winter birds departed as gray arrows out over the sea. I heard them compress the night. Porcelain would chime, books shake from balance, glass cases of floral experiments were battered against the walls. I would stoke the fireplace to blaze off the chill before the couple joined me for breakfast.

Before Rudy began to sleep in our villa Ponchita would watch from the veranda as he fastened his goggles, tromped his thick pedal and disappeared into the fog of the mountain. Though she never cast long looks into the woods after him she would turn on me with the expression of a trapped bird to complain of some remark I had made. She was concerned about his youth and the danger of his companions. Ponchita accused me of denying Rudy the time of day and, in more cryptic terms, of not knowing the difference between fungus and rust. Before he came to live in our villa I would wait at the radio until Ponchita's sounds died away. Then I would ooze delicately into a spot, occupy a foot of the bed, and sleep heavily on sheets that were moist and misshapen. Up hours before her I fluffed out the dish of my skull from the pillow, smoothed away the signs of my body and took coffee in the garden. When finally Rudy drove his trunk and automatic weapon up to our villa I began to occupy as little space as possible, sleeping either beside the garden like a giant among helpless islanders or in my burgundy armchair, padded ears fallen about my neck, legs stretched along my curled dog's back.

I was digging trenches, threading roots, when Rudy's machine crushed my sea-shell drive with its tires. Trunk strapped to his fender and goggles like gleaming peaches he took the slope greedily.

—Do you think your husband will help with the trunk?

I dug about the flowers, lifted them from pots, shook them free of soil, splayed tender roots, and wrapped them until a strong cocoon was made. Ponchita and Rudy were grunting under the weight, fumbling with a broken handle until she screamed and let it fall. My apprentice stood pinned at his ribcage to the iron railing.

—Do something! Ponchita said.

She looked at me with the pinched eyes of a hollow curiosity. I allowed them to lower his goods onto my back and alone I swung the big door wide, alone carried the gooseskin trunk upstairs. Thus I waited, awaiting their quiet steps until Ponchita told me to release it on the sunshine side of the bedroom.

Evenings then became filial, with sherry and cigars enjoyed on the veranda. Ponchita often wore a shirt of mine after her bath. Rudy scratched his scalp or yawned dramatically. It horrified him to make the long silent climb upstairs while I was present. He quietly moaned if, when he removed his shoes, they thudded above my head. Ponchita had instructed him to push aside my clothes in the wardrobe. Yet Rudy would finally leave the veranda, did at last crush out carefully the fire of his cigar, but only as Ponchita and I simultaneously agreed that the time had finally come. She would gaze at him briefly before saying that if they waited too long she would be "useless" in bed.

—And at this time of night I can get Cairo, I added.

For a moment then, after Rudy rolled his fingers at me for a wave, Ponchita and I were alone in the cricket darkness, in the cool air and thrilling rush of leaves. We could be drowsily private. There was still music and dancing, there was terror in the voices on the radio, and my wife remained faithful to Rudy. We would separate on the other side of the door, she energetic suddenly on her way upstairs, I intensely at work fixing the traps against intruders and searching with the ebony knobs for a few words from Cairo.

I went on lighting my torch at night, poking it toward the ruin of my garden. My jungle, citizen: thick, entangled, desperate. To the left of barrowby gems and frail vegas a mound of compost continued to rise to the top of the hedge, at least a foot above the rough red wall. I would balance my flashlight between rocks under the moon and, tumbling to the calluses of my knees, seek with a trowel the crux of a sodbed. Then, in the crisp of night, listening to the insects' constant oring, I would tiptoe to their door and peer in. I would observe by candlelight as they puffed in their sleep, rosy arms around each other, sheets kicked from their nakedness. Two luminous sisters innocent and fearless. From them, despite terror, in the face of nature turning traitor, in the wake of risk and anger—from them I gained confidence.

2

BETWEEN OUR VILLAGE and the next are mountains whose peaks are hidden by clouds. It has been said that at times these peaks have snow on them, or water falling in flakes. If the stories that have been transmitted over many generations are true, a vast plain stretches between the next village and the first of our many cities. We have held festivals for natives who travel to the next village. These begin in gaiety and wonderment as we gather around a table in the Café Kif counting the money the traveler must have to make even the briefest journey—though it will take days—over the mountains. Yet such festivals conclude in fear and sadness. It is as if one of us has died, or has learned of an incurable illness. According to the census the removal of a villager can never be recovered by an additional birth. Also according to the census our village is not the smallest, and though the knowledge is meaningless to us, it is also said that ours is one of the more recent villages.

Every now and then someone will announce his intention to "move" to the city. It is an almost inconceivable journey. We ask how he and his family are going to do that and usually discover an elaborate set of traveling plans involving numerous boats and trains, perhaps even a long journey by hired car in order to reach a bus that will cross the mountains.

As distant as our village lies from the nearest city, the city is still more remote from our capital. In the capital the color of the sea is a matter of conjecture. For us in the village—those who have heard of it at all—the existence of a train that travels under the streets of the capital requires great concentration to imagine. Once I saw a postcard showing a street in the capital, or so the tourist told me who owned it. Ponchita did not believe it was really the capital. She said it had to be Paris or perhaps a city in China. I explained that she was clinging to one of the cracks in our history by denying the capital. That is why I would remember it as spectacular, when the time came, that she had decided to abandon the village and live in the capital. How could she live in a place whose existence she actually doubted? And whose only image came to her through my reports of the news from Cairo?

Of course I have since received a letter from her, a brief one, proving not only the truth of the capital's existence but the authenticity of the postcard. I thought, waving farewell to a steamer loaded with Asians, that Ponchita, who had been terrified by their presence, could not even imagine living in the next village. I would remember however that there had been signs, among which Rudy was only the first.

In our village the population creeps. Our deserted estrademas crowd with natives, when the laws require it, and then we fan into the square around the fountain where a marble squid embraces a naked god. Dwelling in the mountain the bearded goatherds and crumbling grandmothers come with candles and fleas, bearing bundles on carts, riding asses or bicycles with bent rims. Sometimes we have traffic mishaps when poultry and vegetable vans run down dogs in the street. We stand passing wine, sitting on crates or cane chairs to watch our piscators repair torn netting. We discuss and admire the new charms that will be sold when the streets are cluttered and our fat jolly women are paid to pose for photographs. Caids and Pablos and Morgantas skulk below the cathedral doors.

When the sun had seared the fog of a crisp hyacinth morning and Rudy had cut a poisonous ribbon with his motorbike we heard the scream of the bells. Ponchita and I were boiling a rabbit the dog had killed at dawn. At his return the four of us left, locking the shutters against strangers, pushing the dog's angry paw from the rabbit's severed head. Hearing the bells we hurried across the swaying bridge until we saw the prune of the sea against the first white wall of our village. We grasped our friends at their shoulders, I brushed my cheek with Marius. Our baker, a spreading woman in a wide wool dress, licked her thumbs out of habit. We saw her daughter leaning anonymously against the fountain. Adolescent, shy, in a tight sleeveless dress, the baker's daughter discreetly scratched her thigh. I hovered with the dog at the back of the crowd, nervous because of the bulging skirts of the mountain people. The sun angry, vengeful: waxwings looping the cathedral spires like dark threads against the vacuum of the sky: the village, like the clouds, in a bottle. Ponchita's long athletic strides must have frightened the baker's daughter. Between the nodding heads and hard hands of natives forming beasts in the air I caught a glimpse of Ponchita stepping between Rudy and the young girl. Thrusting herself between them Ponchita stood a foot taller than the baker's daughter, her hands were twice as large, her breasts and dancer's legs made the other's seem boyish. The girl could not bear it and averted her eyes, staring suddenly at the palmettos dying on the seashore, dying in the spring. When Ponchita spoke to her she only nodded then looked away where no one waited, where there was nothing to see but the whiteness of our beach, the palmettos, the dry pink bodies of still crabs. And the laws kept a space in the street from the bakery to the fountain where the bells had gathered us.

I do not read lips or minds but, on tiptoe behind the citizens, I understood the significance as a boy with wooly locks handed Ponchita an ice. I spoke of it to the dog while several high-boned natives chiseled holes into the bakery wall. The laws invited us to sing our anthem and the baker lifted her obese flaking hands to begin. Birds flocked, swooped and took crumbs from the gutters. Our language ringing in my ears I watched them bathing on the surface of our fountain water. I watched Rudy seek out Marius then nod to me.

—Did you pay for Ponchita's ice? I tried to ask but he could not hear.

In time to the sound of chiseling and singing Rudy gave a backward glance and started up the road home. I was imagining the silent steps of the baker's daughter as she vanished into the woods to follow him. To these incessancies the sun beat, water poured from the marble squid's tentacles, the workmen blew their breaths into a dozen narrow holes and fingered them for debris. To the tapping halted in the street but taken up in my head the laws stepped officially before us. They pulled the cocks of their weapons. Our singing died away, a few citizens cracked walnuts, and soon there was only the sound of birds and boots on the street.

By the overheard whisper of law to law, the overseen signal of weapons, we trained our eyes on the window above the bakery. What could I do but grip Ponchita's strong claw in mine? Her ice smelled of rain water and fish. She lifted her chin and I pecked her throat.

—A new oven, she said. It will turn the crust black, the way you like it.

She leaned against me with a heavy shoulder, constructing with her hips a circle of disbelief. Ponchita never expressed thoughts, only a convolution of desires and needs. Did she feel the need for guilt? Who but I could have shared her disappointment? I would remember her transparent look of reassurance as the citizens poised breathless as ourselves. We watched workmen heft a small heavy box to the wall of the bakery, watched them draw sticks of dynamite under the guard of men with helmets and face protectors. They slipped explosives into their perfect cradles, attached the threaded fuses. They caulked their precious breathing spaces and surveyed the fingers that dangled a foot along the wall. They might have been planting a rose.

A warplane came off the mountain in the distance, looking first like wreckage against the black ridge. It grew, expanding slim wings until screaming overhead it tilted a glass belly toward us in which a man sat hunched over a weapon. Out over the sea it turned back to pass the coast and the steeples of our village repeatedly. It rattled our teeth. All listened then and munched nuts; Ponchita nibbled a fig. The laws spread their legs, kept visors tipped over faces and covered the length of the street like a wet black smoke. I bent to kiss the coin of Ponchita's vaccination scar.

—What are you after? she said.

Only then could I see into the window, when Ponchita had rejected a celebration with briskets and loins, digging from our trunk the crystal wine goblets. In the window a pair of eyes peeked at the crowd. I saw the flash of a hand as someone went deeper into the room. A shirtless Arab, kerchief around his forehead, lit the fuses one by one with a cigar.

—People, Ponchita whispered.

Above us birds were circling, beside us the laws were nervous as fish. The day had become blinding, a burning day, knee-weakening and windless. I could see far into the sea, could hear the whistle of the hidden warplane. I turned Ponchita's head away when the spunks brightened at their quicks. We were being crushed against the fountain, citizens reeled onto the cathedral steps. The explosives seemed to breathe before they went, drawing into them the noise and air from the street. There were moving figures in the window, then darting again deep into shadows.

A time of salt clay traveling past our heads, of muffled eardrums, of ears rudely covered and jaws distended. In the wave of debris there was a rising of our ancient ruined country, of mountains of lava and the animal ash we had once been. I saw my village, citizen, a flicker in the sea, and at the edge of the explosion young men running, hiding in the time, with pistols in their hands beyond the cold princess of the street and palmettos. By the time the laws realized that the shadows were fugitives crossing sand and shells the shadows had passed the encrusted legs of our promontory and disappeared among our woods. Only after did the laws and citizens turn their heads toward the street again. Ponchita trembled, on his hunkers the dog whined. I petted both with vigorous loyalty. The laws in front of us covered their faces with dark scarves, set Sten guns drooping lazily on their shoulders. I saw the twisted figure of Marius the blind potter seated with a laprobe in his rickety wheelchair in the doorway of the Café Kif.

I paused not because of the law who blocked my passage, nor because of the stark whiteness of our potter's eyes, but in the dust and noise of the waking village I had seen a head jerk itself from the window above the bakery. Laws ordered the head down; they aimed at it. Hair thrown forward the woman crawled as glass burst under her knees. Agnes the prostitute looked quickly but carefully below, gathering details, making a meticulous census of our eyes. Even as the guns moved cautiously to assist her, as a seedy pale blanket was brought into the street and a frightened law pointed his machine at my head, Agnes dropped, crushing hips and forehead without a whimper against the cobbles of the street. They would slide her into a van on a litter. They would discover the nature of her crime. They would provide a vast iron oven for our village. I would remember the blackness of the bread crust and that the time was noon.

I left Ponchita holding the baker's daughter in her arms, touching her eyelids with her lips. The girl had emerged like a wolf from the forest. Rudy I discovered naked on the veranda.

—Agnes, I said.

The shingles were gristed with bees and I watched as one circled Rudy's genitals. I asked him if he had paid for Ponchita's ice. He tipped a wineglass in my direction. And he reminded me, as he danced with Ponchita in the moonlight, of the anonyomous cry that startles the night. I saw in him the lidless eye of the sailor's catch, the heart of the mountain fires. I saw him in the cry of the wild dogs, our priest's fitful sleep, in the village idiot's whimper, the fogged armed streets whose meaning came to me at the sudden silence of the radio. I insisted we bury his weapon in the woods, and we did.

In my dream I was opening our villa door to find that the village and our nut-eyed citizens had disappeared. Our crabswarm had vanished. The sea was at my doorstep, it crossed the threshold and lapped my feet. I explained to Ponchita on the veranda that in this, my first remembered dream, there stood between the villa and the horizon a monstrous gun-blue ship tens of stories high, miles and miles long. I asked her what she thought. She did not answer. I leaned across Rudy in whose arms she lay and saw my wife's puffed stricken face. She was so deeply asleep, like Rudy, and so irrevocably removed from my dream that I could not help but feel relieved. And yet I would have entrusted her with the dream the way ancients used to place rings on the fingers of the dead.

My people say that he who is lean and has scabs need not carry a net: eyes which do not see cannot break a heart: it is worth more to be the head of a mouse than the tail of a lion: the genius in a dwarf is to spit large: each dog who walks finds a bone. Having chewed the peach of disaster I had to smell the barbaric stone. It caused me to wonder whether some person, or group of people, had nourished a hatred of me: a hatred founded perhaps on something as insubstantial as an unreturned greeting or as serious as a personal threat.

I had begun to think that we in the villa had adjusted to our relations with modesty and concern. If I had been observing with the keenness of a mother goat then I might have understood why, when Ponchita ought to have been distraught Rudy was instead, and where he should have been feeling vital it was I who possessed the energy. In the gradual slip of her relations with Rudy I had tried to ease Ponchita's fall. At times I warned my apprentice of danger. But Ponchita, whether in a severe skirt or one of my linen shirts, became more magnificent—her eyes and complexion richer, her body lissom as a butterfly. She too had been warned. I do not know how often I fixed binoculars on the watchtower, on the beach where children had begun to play. Or when it was that I began to meditate in the woods at the pond where goats come to drink and from where they often would run to save their lives. The mystery was that Rudy had begun to suffer. Private tensions which I had only occasionally observed sprang into rueful light, like the bloated louse on the end of my thumb.

—You aren't touching a hair of me, Rudy told Ponchita.

—Do you want them living off you?

Ponchita's shears pinked my earlobes. In my lap I held a basket of hair. Had even our fidelities been stretched too thinly? Was it the news from Cairo that Agnes the prostitute had thrown herself at the wheels of a tractor on the prison farm? It was in part the May heat.

—You are bald as a tomato, Ponchita said. Did you shave yourself?

—Only under the wings, I grumbled.

—That will not do. Next beast.

I had known on that morning that the relations were failing or else I would have been unable to understand their words. When they had shared each other's thoughts they spoke in murmurs, with words so untouched by objects that it seemed they had constructed a symbolic life together. Now, as Rudy walked away toward his vehicle, Ponchita remained, the disenchanted lover whose lyric qualities embarrassed her. We passed a window that reflected our cropped states. On me baldness was a humiliation in which thick clotted veins gave my scalp the look of a surgeon's map. But my wife, having been clipped by me close to the skull, fashioned attractive wavelets of dark hair into the shape of almonds. Seeing ourselves we laughed.

That hot night in the potting shed, my homestead, jars rested with animal parts treated to endure, as did the hanging plants whose enormous leaves brushed my scalp. The dog panted. I stood at the cloudy mirror, studying my body from every possible angle. I was enclosed by an aura of camphor and alcohol, and the moon melted across my rocky head. Invaded hair dissolved in a beaker of acid.

—This is exciting, Ponchita said sprawling on my cot.

—And we've never been hairless together, she added.

Much later, when there was no alternative, after Ponchita had departed for the capital and all relations had lost their ability to surprise, I would remember that we lumbered to the beach, spoke to a nut grower, gave a cigar to a goatherd. It was a thick afternoon, the air was heavy, as if it could be held. The sand was hot where we placed our towels and basket of fruit. Birds on a sand bar fluttered their wings to clear them of dust. Ponchita, in a dark swimsuit with an eyelid of bare flesh at her navel, walked to the sea beside Rudy. I came last with gentle strokes out beyond the breakers. There were, I noticed, fresh wounds on Rudy's back. The dog remained to torment a crab on the beach, to paw it, to prod it with his muzzle. He weaved toward rocks with heavy bounds.

The sea, fierce in our eyes, had intentions. It was an effort to slice it, it returned us to the surface time and again. For a time I listened on my back to the plash of the lovers, and fixed my eyes on the view of our village from the sea. The streets were silent, empty in the hottest part of the day: shutters pulled tight, a dog sleeping in the shade, the grate drawn down at the Café Kif. When I plunged I reached, passing and separating the schools of small fish. I dove erect, arms slowly drawing in, toes pointed like rubber fins until I could feel the cold shimmer of undercurrent. And then I arched backward, weaving a vague circle that allowed me to see ribbons of air I had just expelled. In our sea human skin glows. Plants have the feel of fresh kidneys when you grasp them in your hands. The silence has an odor.

Heavy as a treasure I fell profoundly, to the point of being without rescue. The creamy action of movement at the surface brought a tightening in my throat. Drifting on the floor of our sea, fauna alone around me, I drew a curtain across my vision. I remained, unrooted, now and again tossed as the force of a wave pressed to the bottom. I let air escape once, twice, heard I thought the bark of a dog pierce the curtain, felt in my stomach the nausea I feel below a night full of stars. Then suddenly the speckled texture of the sea, like stars against a black smoky sky, left a metallic taste in my mouth. A taste of poison or rust. I had never before ventured so deep. All fish swam above. The bones of a diver lay scattered among a cluster of rocks, in the weed bed of sharp coral. I touched a bone, brought it to my mouth, then did nothing but feel the wood of it. I searched for the skull but could not find one.

It was as I poised my hands upon living sponges that a fume shot by in a stream or pellet. On a wave that began from the floor I rose against my will, a fist at my throat, and saw fish being raised by their fins in front of me, eyes bugging, their gills puffy as mine. I thought I saw a wreck in the corner of my sight, a barnacled horror that I would not have touched. The sea broke painfully in my ears, the sun burst against me like a sore, and there was a hiss, the sound of hot metal dropped in ice. Rudy stood to the waist near the shore, his arms urging me in. I waved back in a dizziness that erased all sense of having touched the bottom, of having looked among the sponges. Ponchita bounced toward me, her breasts seeming fuller than I had remembered; the dog in terror splashed as far as Rudy. The roar of engines knocked me from my aching stroke, made me afraid to look back. Instead I aimed at Rudy's hand, and drove with all my strength into his arms. I fell into the lap of Ponchita's hysteria.

Behind us the gray mass, boiling in bright coils of flame, sent snapping sounds into the air. Its hull tipped down the tail stood twenty feet tall, like a building impervious to the sea. An orange flotation overcame a wave, and we saw goggles, a leather jacket, weighing with sea until they disappeared. We observed the spinning tail section break off and cut across the surface. The rotor blades touched down with a searing cry. I saw a number, my country's flag, a bushy head vanish in the gulp of an echo. After we had swum into the debris with cautious loggy strokes Rudy gripped the pilot by the chin while I tossed off the leather cap. His hot breath warmed my ear when I turned him gently toward shore. I cushioned his beard in my hand, rubbed his tangled mat of hair which still smelled of sweat from the cap. Turning from

Rudy I held him against the ocean, placed two fingers in his mouth to clear it of blood. The sea was carrying us easily though I heaved my lungs to keep our heads high. When he twisted against my hand I thought it was Rudy taking hold. But then a wetness thicker than seawrack covered my chest. For a few strokes I went on, until Rudy swam forward to seal the way.

—Let him go, he said.

My hands and chest were bloody. When I raised the pilot by the head I could see the jagged slash marks that had exposed his vocals, low, in the valley above his heart, where food begins to digest even as it is swallowed. Still I held him, rubbing to smoothness a gray ratted sideburn.

—Blades, Rudy said.

The skin of his throat torn open, the pilot's head throbbed against me in even heavy butts. I held him face down in the sea and slowly pushed away. His heavy mountain boots drew him under. We swam at first slowly, then churning and raising foam in leaps behind us. Gulls swooped nearby, the dog galloped from rocks to the edge of the water. Shutters flew open and citizens began to rush from their afternoon beds. We were hurrying to Ponchita who had already gathered our towels and basket, whose lovely fear and confusion caused me to pause on the beach.

The gleam of our rocks and limbs of our trees hid our escape. The goatherd in his dark rags nodded but did not speak. The village seen through binoculars from the roof of my villa was crowded, noisy, dangerous, though it was a blistering afternoon. I felt the itch of a caterpillar as it traveled my leg. A storm was whistling down the coast, the laws moved to disperse the crowd. Together we trembled until darkness brought calm. There was calm, darkness, the thunder of fists against metal in my dream.

They brought dogs to sniff out the flyer if by chance he had been washed onto the rocks of a grotto or had drifted during the night into the kelp waters. Yet hounds covered the village and woods too, during empty sweltering days, but found nothing human. Only then did Rudy scrutinize me, forming questions with his eyes. He would return to the veranda in a robe after Ponchita had gone to sleep, clearing his throat of uncertainty. Or arrive at the foot of my cot in the potting shed, after Cairo had been scrambled from the radio, and there watch me under the light of a dull bulb. He inspected my shelves, squinting through murky rich liquids. There were sacs of skin under his eyes, the track of a fear wrinkle at the bridge of his nose. He wore a pasty medicine over a pimple on his forehead and his fingernails had no pink left. I watched a maroon scab encrust the muscle of his calf.

The night air could still bite and our footfalls on the shells of my drive echoed, made us tend to tiptoe when we walked into the woods. I led him with a torch through the garden, over the wall, into tall weed and lush grass. At times we sat on rocks as smooth as headstones. The sky settled a misty blue film over the landscape, giving the still water of the pond a creamy light. I kept us from the edge, hidden by the boughs of the banana trees. Rudy was nervous being alone with me in the woods: a pitiless bird screech reached us from the watchtower: the skins of bananas glimmered, as if we could see deeply, clearly into their systems. We watched a goat tongue the pond, causing a blossom to ripple in our direction. She ate wildflowers and snorted. She gathered her young who, lapping water in the silence before dawn, sounded as if they were beside us.

We watched the goats scamper away, hooves kicking high behind them, and we stretched ourselves in the high weeds at the sound of crushed twigs. Rudy fled like a shrew into the mountain as the laws carried torches and automatic weapons into the woods. I saw Rudy hunker near them, then saw him climb steep slopes without a sound. I squatted, assuming one of the positions Ponchita had grown to dislike: chin in hand, elbows on knees, lying in wait for any sudden storm to pass. Only after that, standing beside my cot, knotting the ends of his robe sash, did Rudy study my beakers and find the courage to ask about my sealed jars. And only then, witnessing the nightly hunt of the laws, could Rudy ask me not to betray him.

The flyer was spotted by a child pointing lazily along the beach. Swimmers who had searched returned alone because the body was too poisonous and teeming with sea life to be handled. Natives came to watch when a gunboat whistled and a lowered hook caught the flyer around the middle. An arm had broken behind the flyer's neck and would not straighten. When the corpse was raised by a hoist, sea water poured from it. We saw it shrink, like a punctured blowfish, while spinning slowly in the air it disgorged eels and weed. The swimmers battered fish back into the sea.

Behind thin fig branches Ponchita and I saw the huge corpse, the hair in motion as it rose from the sea. We waited until the beach was cleared and the laws moved aimlessly through the village. We noticed for the first time the tread of a tank in the sand. Ponchita was anxious to tell Rudy and I left them alone to talk. Late that day I heard the fierce yapping of dogs in the woods above the garden. They were coming down off the mountain. With Ponchita and Rudy in bed I peered over the garden wall expecting to watch the laws arrive in a troop formation.

But these were different dogs, mixed breeds, wild and growling, with murder on their minds. I saw them in pursuit, and then at the crest of a hill, traced against the setting sun, the she-goat they had outrun. She still climbed, head bent, tongue swollen, when two of the dogs bit cleanly through the tendon of her hind leg. The goat collapsed on her chin, making an effort to rise even though reeds of muscle were being peeled to the ground. The pack raced upon them and the she-goat was alive when they drove their muzzles into her belly. They barked, howled, then were quiet, and the horizon had become the color of the sea. I had to hold my dog back to keep him from running with the others.

3

WHAT AMOUNT of pleasure had it been to construct a garden in the mountain? Had my hopes been as fulfilled when I witnessed its growth and decay as when I had designed it? Why had I chosen so sublime a task for myself? Ponchita, then Rudy, posed such questions to me, yet always in the form of criticism, always as an accusation of tending the progress of mortification. From their places in the sun they would stare at my labor, warn me of an arriving lizard, then pose questions to which they did not expect an answer. I would tell them that as far back as my memory stretched, avenue of the rich to the shocking white villa—all now crushed into a few traumatic moments—I used to kneel in the soil at midnight, feeling my way with delicate fingers until drawn by scent I would return one small furrow of ground to beauty. And this, I informed them, reminded me of decorating my mother's and then my wife's birthday cakes: from the blank object exuding its vacuum before me it became the splendor of truth: the sticky green swirl, the sugar dotted i: *Happy Birthday Sweetheart.*

Were they satisfied? Could they leave my dedication where it belonged? And so I would tell them that beyond the anarchy a successful garden requires and the concern for detail that such disorder exacts there is also a sense, a floral sense. If not logic, pattern. I for one would love to have ballet girls through the winter but they cannot be kept. I have tried, I watched them die. I can however lift a happy hand to winter jasmine, fix a meaningful glance on honeysuckle, on columbine. A path, like mine, is made mellow with pansies and chiendents, they crop as they will, here and there, very like the accident of a splendid gathering of friends. What are the lessons of this sense, the floral sense? Would Ponchita and Rudy ask, or did I have to lead them to it?

They touched toes when I spoke against herboriums, against use value—the eating of your garden, the smoking of its beauty. It is floral sense to stagger color, to erect beside the threshold beds a summer seat of granite in order to hear the chanting among blossoms. It is floral sense to respond to the laughing face, mouth open in a bow, of the doreen dow, and to acknowledge the efforts of Puschkinia to achieve its pine cone shape, the Madame Pompadours their droop. To realize that there is exquisite grace in the leek. To contemplate, and make fruitful by its absence, the wine of primrose, of callas, cowslip.

Had they noticed, creaming their legs with oil, the nature of auricula: the terror in the pupils, the fingernail rivers coursing the meat of the flower? Nothing in fertilizing history, or theory, has ever changed: attack succubae that insinuate in the roots: winter remains the Borgia of plant life. How would Ponchita have enjoyed the authority of the red-hot pokers that hedged my rough wall? How Rudy might have blossomed among the daphnes I kept to myself. As fear was the skin of passion, truth was its pit, together they composed a fruit—my Ponchita, her Rudy. The rose, the lotus, I explained, were for themselves. They were not I digging around them or touching an underleaf. They had futures, they would grow in ash and in lava. And if love was truth's left breast, novelty its right, where had the lovers gone when I looked up at their vacant chairs with a smile? They had failed to notice the dahlia's allegory.

Aucuba, aggressive laurel, rockery wives. The rose excels in its bed, is superb upon any wall, glorifies the arbor and the arch. Carmine pillar, crimson rambler. I could talk then of Hector's helmet, Achilles' shield. Of sunburst tea and Maréchal Niel after pruning. The rose, once white, a goddess had bled upon, giving us monthlies, then perpetuals. Yet I hoed only to find aphides, green humming flies. I saw frog hoppers, sawfly grubs, cockchafers, miners, black spot, scorch, bedeguar. I cried to Rudy, called for the knife, the tar, the grab! *Schnell*, I cried! We unwound the hose and I indicated coltsfoot and groundsel. I told him to do his duty or I would throw him down the mountain. Remember, Rudy, I know where you sleep, I will not hesitate to come for you. Do it, I growled, do it! *Schnell*, *schnell*, *schnell*!

When next I saw Rudy—I would remember it from the parapet of our cathedral—he looked like a seal. Ponchita was again in the village, though this time I had encouraged her myself. She was to sweep then scrub our stall while I completed my potting in the garden. Cruise ships were already at anchor, and low sporty autos made our streets impassable when I watched her depart, like a peasant and weary wife, with bucket, broom and horsehair brush. Rudy must have been hiding nearby because soon after my wife disappeared his motorbike skidded across my shells which looked from the garden like millions of discarded ears.

He was dressed in a shining leather suit that stretched the length of his body and was tucked at the bottom into black high boots. A thick silver chain crossed his chest from the shoulder of one arm to the ribcage below the other. I carried pots buffed white as day, then unpotted roses weighted with clods of dirt. I arranged in neat rows the sprays of flowers that had survived, arranged them in the low wooden cart which my dog was to pull down the mountain.

—Are you happier now? I said to Rudy.

We stood in the sunshine squeezing eyes at each other, his tightly narrow, until the raven chest of him gave wind to a huge sigh. He looked away, young again, blue eyes strong as the marble sky. Perhaps he thought I was prosperous. Perhaps he did not understand the smothering ragweed, the world of bees and shells, the smell of alcohol on my clothes. He must have thought he had been betrayed.

I began to push my loaded cart toward the dog in harness, inhaling the aroma I was providing our village. I heard his rapid bootsteps but did not turn to look. When he shoved me aside and tipped the cart roses fell from the corners of my eyes, we heard the ringing of pottery as it broke upon the shells, as he dashed it with his heel. And we saw the collapsing of the cart's bent wheel as it snapped and came apart like a wafer.

The rose man gathered himself from the ground, no more interested in dusting himself or straightening his white linen suit than a fallen horse. With utmost concentration I began to pick crushed petals out of the debris. Rudy faced me but I passed by. I watched him mount his grisly machine. With the thunder of breaking glass and a violent yet painful wave Rudy left the villa for good. When Ponchita returned, hours later, I did not tell her of Rudy's violence. But, she said, to find me plugged into the radio in the middle of the day, when tourists were combing the village, when Marius was keeping my chair in the Café Kif—was it an aftertaste of anger or lust she saw in my eyes? I asked her then for the first time what it was she did so often in the village. What it was that was happening in the shadow of the cathedral spires. Whom she was seeing between our fountain and our first white wall. She only drew her knees together and rocked at my side.

Imagine the change in the sea when I observed it from the roof of the villa between the fragrant banana trees. I was crouched on the tiles, binoculars strapped to my neck. Unbroken waves rolled beyond the black leg of the coast: blue calm drifted toward the oil of our fish run: a departing steamer fumed at the horizon: squid boats nested in coves or motored gently out from shore. I saw a beast break the sea glass. When I considered the natural differences among us I felt a dark private peace and the cold shoulder of a personal doom. It was not youth Ponchita spoke of when finally she left me, I maintain my youth in every springy step, each active glance. I understood her need, felt too the distance between us. For me distance had been at the center. Perhaps, then, I had urged it.

At the time she did not mention the capital and I do not think she yet believed in it. She merely packed two leather cases and walked slowly enough to the village so that I could see her through the binoculars for several minutes. I saw her stop to pick an orange, saw her change the cases from one hand to the other. I watched her step quickly over the swaying bridge. I would remember, citizen, how we had first come up, had pushed the cart now destroyed but then filled with cases and crates, how we had stopped to retrieve a puppy that cowered beside the road. What was I then? More a son than a husband? Ponchita would stare at me over meals wondering what it had been like in the avenue of the rich, and to have remained so long in my mother's hermitage.

Did I admit to her that I used to unlace my sneakers on Mother's stairwell after a grudging day in our garden? Or that before I could walk the esplanade to the casino I had to sit with Mother in the parlor over teacups of rum and watch her gouge at toenails with a scissors? I would puff my cigar in the direction of her foot. The foot stank. And I would lift my own feet to the windowsill, observing rooftops along the avenue of the rich grow yellow and shadowy as the evening light cast a lull. Autos parked, wash taken in, lamplights bright in kitchen windows, no prospect of war or riot.

Even later in our marriage I never mentioned that Mother's head, which sloped like an egg, was tan from the sun, and that her skull was brittle as if, along with her hair, it had thinned. In our tool shed I created the image for her of a master carpenter, my thick forearm swinging steady as a pendulum against knotty pine and oak, driving cooper or clouthead nails into fragrant slabs of wood. Mother must have been fixed by the closed left eye when I hammered, by my squinting right eye when, with a stodgy hip motion, I sawed through a timber. There would be wood shavings on her sweaters as she watched sawdust gather on both our shoes. She would share her cigarette in our tool shed, roll up her trouser leg above the ankle to deposit our ashes in the crease. Often she kept talking, I sawing, she rolling trouser legs until her shins were visible and seemed to glow like new wood itself. She would make me tear myself from her presence.

Mother's room remained clouded with dust and yet smelled of oil. For it I built a credenza, a wardrobe, a dais covered with swanskin. Near the end I was constructing a pergola in our garden for the clematis to grow upon. A gibbet I left in the shed because Mother said it was too like a guillotine. Her face could sag, fall into dark moony expressions; or, after I had explained why I had to leave the house, she would slant her violet eyes with fingers the color of tobacco and say:

—Tall boy's excuses, like skin of sensitive maid, very very thin.

Would it have been worthwhile to tell Ponchita that I could stare at Mother, and she at me, for hours from armchairs across the room? Or that, having told a funny story to her, we would repeat the joke of it whenever we passed each other in the house or garden? I made clown faces at her, and if she did not laugh then I made hideous faces, pulling the muscles of my lips over each other until I puckered like the fish we had just eaten. At last I would gaze at her closed door, noticing that the wrinkle of light under it meant she was reading an imported mystery. Only then was I able to stalk the night in search of a crowd, not the crowd I would later associate with strikers' nights, fire riots, earth tremor panic, with obsessive chants or smoke in the moonlight rising from the eye of a rifle.

The shriveled skins of Venetian lanterns lit terraces on both sides of the esplanade. Shops and kiosks were shut for the day: ribbed grates like accordions hid jewels, fashions, linens behind huge padlocks chained and chained again against intruders in the avenue of the rich. I could hear the first of the search planes high and secret in still clouds. Past the movie house, the night spots and dance hall, one of the laws would place a thick hand on my arm to remind me that once at the bottom of the long stone staircase I would no longer be in the avenue of the rich. At the edge of the esplanade the sound of the tide against boats moored in the harbor was obliterated, eaten by the noise of smoky native cafés. With my eyes wider than deserts I would enter the fog of the casino to view the woman who danced interpretive.

I liked walls where my shoulders could feel them. I saw blonde people with brown skins and luminous outfits leave the dance floor at the roll of a drum. All the rest Ponchita knew. That when she stepped to the stage I was there applauding the rose in her hair or the fan at the widow's peak. The trumpet was soft, in the darkness behind her I could see the flash of a hand that played the guitar, the spunk of the drummer's cigarette. Her fingers snapped with deliberateness, sounding like coins touching. A single curl fell slick against her forehead and two hooped rings bobbed from her ears. I never saw her teeth because of the lipstick she applied in thick bright layers. Like the sweat and the refusal to smile, or raising her arms to reveal the muscles she had made of her breasts, the abrupt stomp of wooden shoes that ended her performance was an indication of earnestness. With a gesture almost of defiance she was gone before the applause began.

Only later, after she had nodded to me with a presumption of intimacy between us, after I had pursued her like a child under a piano seeks a frightened cat, did Ponchita, parting strands of hair from her face, admit she wanted sex with me but never a child. So it was she who reminded me that I had spoken one night of a subtle but substantial difference between the spider dying and the spider dying of love. When she remembered this I admitted that Marius the blind potter had said it was a construction that might affect her deeply.

It was a time when I could stand in our garden, Mother's and mine, to wait for signals from the mountain as if it were a planet millions of light years distant: when I walked the village streets with an arm looped through Caid's and sat for the first time in the Café Kif with Marius imparting knowledge: when returning home, past the Arab alleys, up the long stairs became a hunch growing on my back, crushing thorax against lungs, putting stomach and heart together against my ribs. I would sag finally into the mattress of my bed, gaze sickly around the room at a web in a corner where a moth hung annealed, at a calender on the wall in which a woman in furs reclined on a rock, at the door marked by darts on which a sliver of wood betrayed the fact that Mother had removed the lock.

Perhaps I spoke too often of finding the shutter drawn in Mother's room late one night. The breeze had whistled through it. As I turned toward her bed I was held by the small jewel on a chain which had always been buried in a dress or blouse. The jewel had no meaning for me except that it shone against her arm, twisted as the chain was around her throat. Dawn was threatening. Mother's eyes remained open, I closed them. Her arms were uncoiled above her head, thrown back, as if she had leaped out from under the quilt. Her arms were heavy as taffy, a rich maple color at the creases of her elbow. In opposing directions her great breasts tilted, flat and girlish because her body was so stiffly arched, like the neck of a swan. The bodice of her nightgown had fallen to her waist and with the hem of it lifted I saw her legs slightly separated, saw a handful of smoky aged hair along her thighs.

I watched myself in her mirror as I studied the room, returning always to her body. Her mouth, citizen, lay open, hollow, black. Her false teeth were rocking from her gums; reaching with two fingers between her lips I jerked the plate loose and put it in my pocket. I lit one of the perfumed candles and left. My second visit to the death room came in the early light after I had rested in my undershorts outside her door. I rocked in a chair, smoked a cigar, thought of Mother having seemed ageless as a tortoise. I noticed in this visit that a slipper fluttered on the end of her toe and that the shelf above the bed had collapsed, dumping the feathery ashes of dead pets from their urns. I brushed ash from Mother's shoulder and felt careless that I had overlooked it: her shoulders had never lost their youth—they were soft, pale, unblemished. In the rocker outside her door I lit another cigar, smoking while I gazed at the bear cub of stars in the dissolving gray sky. I tracked its disappearance into the day. I thought I heard tapping somewhere in the house.

During the next visit I no longer trembled or found myself waiting to catch wind. She had swallowed a glass of gelatin to restore nails: a dish and spoon stood by the window—she had eaten looking down into the village: a matchbox was empty in a wicker chair, an ashtray full. After breakfast I went in again, thinking of Mother's consistency, touching nothing in the room. I turned my back then on the ashlar and flint smell, showered, packed a leather case and left in the windless early autumn. There was such a day when I watched from the doorway of the Café Kif, an arm around Marius, until Mother's body was brought down into the village and our garden went to ruin. In my hand her teeth were like little windows or wash on a line. I held them before the potter's useless eyes. He called them bare behinds in the prison shower. Did Ponchita realize that one of the leather cases she took with her had belonged to my mother? Even I did not recall until she struggled with it over the bridge.

Against the walls of the village from its place above the sea the sun appeared oily and drew an outline of our buildings in violet and kelp green. Doves, swallows hovered and swooped. Vendors with large voices hawked before the Café Kif where at night one could dance and drink. Foreigners arrived in ships that dwarfed the village. Men wore white boaters, women with porcelain faces held onto blowing mushroom hats. I was touched by the absence of flowers. Though it left me at an agonizing threshold their absence signaled the natural doom for a life of beauty and soft rubies. Perhaps it was accidental that a goat wandered into my garden, or that next day a fox arrived to horrify my dog. But unless I was prepared to sink into revery, conjure luckless memories without scrutiny I had to admit to the newer sphere I could enter.

The village, I sensed, was spinning an inexorable yet infinite net. I had helped tend it, not as a weaver or artisan, or as a gunman for the law. I would tend it even now by lacing my sneakers high, tight, gathering hemp in coils from the potting shed, fashioning traps I had once used to disarm intruders in my villa to make them valuable in the woods. I returned to the pond where the laws had been prowling, returned near dawn where I had sat with Rudy, and after patient attention snared the she-goat I had spied at midnight. Her kids followed in a string. With binoculars I followed the movements of sheep as they studied the grass below the watchtower. I snared them, and the fox that had followed. I found a cormorant in my trap in a tree, a shrew in its nest against the mountain. I listened for the dogs and beat them to their prey. When I perked coffee, shaved the stubble from my head, I was able to observe the various motions of creatures leashed to the veranda, to the table in the kitchen, or caged in roomy quarters bedded with straw.

The sounds, citizen, were tremendous. The smells could take my breath away. They grumbled while I ate among them, left on occasion mysterious droppings that could not be identified—had another animal wandered in without my knowing? I do not wish to say they were playful but they were not at least lethargic. Only the lobster was an error; finally it had to be eaten and this unnerved the rest. They watched in silence as I plunged it into a boiling kettle. They took comfort in the radio and kept their tempers, after a time, because of the oversight of the dog. The dog grew attached to my labor and never faltered in his duty toward the animals. From them I took wool, milk, eggs. They were fed, warmed and exercised. Only once was I attacked and that was while the shrew was giving birth, in itself not a lovely sight. Time and again I nuzzled into the flanks of the she-goat, the sheep, spoke until they listened, or seemed to, to the birds and skitterish game. I brought a mole a trough of soil from the garden, wishing only for more exotic creatures to find.

I climbed a nut tree for a new owl and carried it like an egg into the villa. I waited for days, seeing owls course past the windows, peering in on slanted wings. They entered on their own, perching on the furniture, clearing throats during the night. House snorting while I made coffee and removed pellets from the oats and hay I came to be expected. At the violent rise of subsequent mornings the animals brayed, wet, cooed and wailed. Foliage soaked in the roaring sun.

It is said that in certain tropical zones there live people who shrink the heads of their enemies and fill them with sand: in other places snails four feet long sleep in the shade provided by hundreds of deadly snakes coiled above them in the branches of trees: elsewhere men, I have heard, eat buses: something called voodoo is no laughing matter. These things, and more like them, have fused at a dubious moment into implications. When the time came I would remember, facing the animals who chewed so calmly near my feet, that such oddities formed the magic, the uniqueness of all natural activity, and that such magic deserved thought. If I considered these things as forms of magic I also concluded that all of them shared a common element: there could be no magic where there was no audience: magic, or uniqueness, could not exist even as an idea without people to observe it, people who in reluctance or delight are mystified and made to feel safer knowing there remain things that confuse our morality and fire imagination.

I understood these things on the day my dog barked drum beats into the slick wrapper on which his dinner lay raw and bloody. After Ponchita had been absent from my sight for more than a week. I learned that there are warm places where flies have lost their buzz and cold countries where water life has been trained to plant and trigger bombs. I was constantly in touch with foreign voices. The dog, arching himself as he tore bed linen and upholstery in his teeth, gnawed through the legs of chairs and my holiday shoes with what seemed the aching fangs of a viper. I was feeling so unusual that fresh breezy morning—as if I could unzip my spine, unscrew my testicles like blackened light bulbs—that I considered raising a beard to emphasize the smooth sleek rest of me. I considered the appearance of worms that seemed to travel beneath the skin of my naked head when I shaved it.

From the edge of the veranda I saw through binoculars that a ship had anchored and the streets were as resplendent as the flesh of sunbathers in their daring holiday swimwear. My white suit I brushed to a high gloss. Sneakers I whitened with the polish Ponchita often used on her nails and, tilting my cream hat at a dangerous angle, I went whistling down to the crowd. What exactly does the audience do when it watches its healing priests, its faith mongers? When it observes the sudden brooking of a curative spring, the rabbit yanked from a shiny topper? Does it not finally verify the illusory nature of mystery itself? Does it not merge two perfectly recognizable aspects of reality—rabbits and hats—and agree in self-dialogue that since we do not ordinarily see rabbits inside hats or fountains bursting from rock that a miracle has occurred? Is miracle the occasion when we safely join terror and joy? Is that all, Ponchita, it takes to keep the citizens still? Rabbits, white gloves, satin tunnels down which you are not permitted to look?

A day after the cruise ship came bleating around our promontory Marius the blind potter was arrested.

4

DAYS OF INTERROGATION may be as marked by dreariness as they are by torture. In spite of pain, regardless of a sincere disgust shared by inquisitor and questioned, irrevocable ties are known to have been made. Strapped to a chair, face welted black, nose crushed to a porridge, one may yet receive a glass of water to rinse out the blood from split gums. With eyes closed and lids swollen as mountains one may ask to have his throat slit and by the request feel he is making a special contact. The laws leave tattoos in cheeks and groins.

With my ear to a pillow I could hear depths of invisible speech, I saw a fluffy donkey coming down the road. At such a moment the propeller beats of warplanes were only cuffs against silence. If it could be in the village square that I die I would take the silence with me, drain it from the noise of carts and cocking guns, and at the moment I fell I would enter a fissure of truth, leave behind chatter, rumor, slander. When the blindfold had been removed and the bullets pried from my head only clouds of quiet would flow. Unheard speech pour from my mouth, images snap from my riddled skull. Such images would seal fate. I would have been an explosion in the day, splitting corrupt silence: the moment before the dynamite blows: breath held before the shot is fired: a ghost of sound dead in the square fragmenting the speeches that follow.

Amid catacomb footsteps the breath of the pickpocket and the touch of a finger that leaves no print is fearsome. Plots are being hatched, others dug. These images I held in a cup of thought as a weapon. I had awakened to find teeth marks along my arm, blood dots on the meaty underwidth, the part that retains the skin of a baby. I swung the arm to my face, parting the shutters for new light with the other. Bathers streamed toward the beach. My teeth fit perfectly into the bruise. Was it because I possessed no genius that I seemed less likely to be revealed?

I took up binoculars once again and looked along the road into the village. The bridge had been set into a melodious roll. A glint of metal struck my eye, a rise of dust halfway down the mountain. I heard the piu-piu-piu of gunburst. When I left the villa I had in mind the automatic weapon Rudy and I had buried in the woods. But the laws would come, I thought, with such confidence that they would not sneak or surround my villa. I looked for them along the road, expected to see them marching or alighting from trees, guns on hipbones, gossiping to each other.

There was instead a burro bleeding in the road, and as I walked toward it my hands were clasped behind my head in a gesture of absolute capitulation. My face bore a look of exoneration. I searched the camouflage of brush for the gunmen, stared into treetops lined with snipers like anxious crows, stepped into the ravine that would be jammed like a mass grave with trigger-mad young natives. I halted in the midst of it, letting dust kiss my sneakers and listening to flies that swarmed the burro's body. I always knew I would stand one day, remain waiting in such a ravine and posture, squinting with one eye because of the gleam of metal against the sun.

It was no trial of conviction that while standing in the hot sickening road beside the stench of dead flesh, with arms straining, as if shackled already, so there could be no misjudgment about my surrender, I rolled original thoughts in my brain. I imagined their assault on the villa by door and windows, their astonishment at the condition of my house, their disgust at my filled space, at the jars and beakers and reeking livestock. I wished to submit, made the cowering gesture, but was neither repentant nor vengeful. They would merely be doing what it is they do, and I the same.

By the time, citizen, the dream of capitulation plumped my imagination I was staring with certainty from arm to ravine, mimosa to tall brush and had lowered my hands. I went closer to the burro, saw that it had been drilled with bullets and then saw near it the wheels of the motorbike still spinning. Chrome spokes were bent, shining. Abandoned and injured beyond repair—a space in its chest from which fuel leaked—the machine lay riderless. What remained was the nearly explainable element that after a few moments of meditation, while gathering dust and flies near the road, I lit a cigar, puffed it to a bright heat and tossed it into the sea of fuel. The torso of the motorbike exploded instantly, forcing me to set my teeth. The flames took with them the leather bags behind the rider's seat, the rubber of the tires, the face and then the body of the burro. From my roof into the night I watched natives and laws gather at the spot, observing the ground burn black. None of them moved to douse the fire and I could see the intensity of their faces in its light. The smoke tumbled toward the sea, traveling in what seemed a thunder out to the liners in the harbor where tourists stood on deck to witness.

I tended the livestock sullenly, brooking no complaints. The dog and I ate on the veranda in the dark, admiring old photographs, wrestling on the shells before bed. A tremor caused me to fall. Voices from Cairo came in waves, beginning at midnight and returning until dawn. The night grew, it would not stop brooding. It sent me to the garden with cramps like pins where lizards, it seemed, clawed out of my body under the moon. Near sunrise, more tremors.

Soon I would be remembering that one day, next to the unplugged gramophone, a small birdcage would sit, and in it a pair of budgies staring at themselves in a mirror. They would gently rock on a wooden perch, ring a bell with their beaks. The birds sang me into the room where owls watched them dubiously and the fox sniffed their bars. I affirmed to the creatures that the birds were not ours, that neither the dog nor I was responsible for their presence. Their fragility and short rapid heartbeats had no part in the arrangement of things. I would only smile. The dog left the villa unhappily. And I could have called out the name but I chose instead, acknowledging the sign, to uncork a white wine bottle and search for her. I knew of course where she must be waiting. The animals followed me from room to room as far as the leashes could stretch. Together we drank in the anticipation of missing her each time. With the musty cork in my teeth, sharp animal nails prancing the wooden floor behind me, I nourished the thought that Ponchita was but a few steps ahead, her sandals kicked off, darting from sunburst to shadow and repressing one of her enormous laughs.

The texture of wood rises at such a moment, when you creep along the staircase, leaving your livestock to watch from the bottom. I had to place fingers at my lips to keep from speaking. When arch and sneakers were one, and I felt firmly conciliatory, I quietly began to hum one of Ponchita's favorite songs. After I had entered the room to hear breath being sucked I was struck at first, instinctively, by my largeness and her diminution. The hairy dark skin, for example, of my forearm next to which the girl's thigh was no match. Her face froze when I came at them across a ribbon of sunset on the bed. The terror of her expression was enhanced by the maculation that was pale, the color of soft plum, on her cheek. Their legs parted when I intruded and the baker's daughter pretended that the sharp elbows, the heaving rib-cage, the formidable nipples of the flat chest were not really her own. After I had pulled up a chair Ponchita could do no less than sigh like a wounded deer, lean glassy-eyed into the girl's face and, with neither pretense nor diversion, remove her arms from the body.

—Open your eyes, she said to the baker's daughter.

—It's time you met.

—Fumée, this is my husband.

Fumée would be stranded on her pillow, marooned in the goose feather smell. She cupped her ears. Ponchita insinuated that I resembled a fungus, and admitted she had thought when she entered the villa that I had abandoned it, gone into the mountains, to one of the camps. The cork was still in my mouth so I did not reply. I learned from Ponchita that something infinitely chalky had happened to my skin. Fumée began to grunt so I placed a sheet across her body. Ponchita and I could trust each other because there was a witness. I suggested bouillabaise to go with the wine, and the girl jumped out of bed to make it. I told her not to mind the shrews. She looked at me as if this were another planet, if there were another planet.

Animal noises must have greeted the girl downstairs because we would hear her curse at the top of her voice. Ponchita described the arrest of Marius, how the laws drove up in a van and carried him into it, leaving the wheelchair behind though she herself had rushed it to them. There was no more Café Kif. I stiffened as she mentioned the capital: the flaming motorbike had made her believe in it. We were silent and went to the window. I could see the curve of her lashes, the plump thumb of her earlobe. The swelling of her pelvis drew the sun. We were past touching. And I was being plagued by dreams. Could she believe it? I explained that I had come to trust them and that, on their behalf, since we would not see each other again, I had several requests.

—Please do not accept the attentions of a wall-eyed man smoking through an onyx holder. Also, avoid driving low cars through the mountains. Do not wander at sunset into any open field if you see a windmill and a farmer leaning on a rake at the horizon. When winter arrives do not purchase anything electrical to warm you because it will short circuit but you will be too soundly asleep to notice. Perhaps, though, it will be some comfort to learn that you will be sleeping alone if this happens. Avoid these things and I believe your life will see you well.

Then I offered to contribute toward a surgery that might remove Fumée's strawberry. I was willing in fact to contribute skin if it became necessary. Ponchita said that it was impossible to remain in the village after the flaming motorbike.

—In fact dinner is a bit ridiculous.

Though I wanted to remain with her at the window I would leave her standing and go quietly downstairs, put a stop to the bouillabaise. I had been standing at the motorbike —I have pieced it together a thousand times since—weak in the knees and bladder. I had always hated that motorbike. It was leaking fuel, an illusion of stillness informed the spinning wheel, Rudy's chain belt was tangled around the headlamp. It had got what it deserved. The motorbike would not get up again. Like all machines, I thought, it is human.

The charm of the placid sea, the warm powdery feel of beach as a hundred pairs of feet sank into it and pressed the air around them. Tourists had tottered lamely into the cathedral where the cleric unlatched the dowel to the ancient tombs, murmuring at them to watch steps. Hippodrome faces, gargoyles with hooves, marble orcs for eyeballs: behind an ivory ectoplasm in a corner the reliquary of our saint: his spleen dried to a prune, tongue pressed flat, our saint's skin was thin as rice paper. I waited, as did the village, for the cruise ship to depart, leave us our ceremonies. A child, a leg brace that sang like piano keys on the floor. The tourists sensed our anxiety and breathed rooty barreling heaves as the doors taller than ten men boomed shut behind them. Sunlight slipped in at the tomb window. I was at last moved to hear our cleric pumping and pounding his faith at our six-hundred-pipe organ manufactured by Swedes. The tourists would touch gingerly as moths the peacock blue of robed statuary, the hard crimson lips, the white aspects of death masks. They would read our horror stories in each stained glass.

What else could I have done other than enter the cathedral bulwark where power and history had lain siege? Here water was boiling beside the evangelistary, the copper kettle spit an oriental vapor into the air. Waiting for the priest I stood above the village in the wind of the parapet. Even without binoculars I could see beyond the marble squid as a black sedan slowly moved into the street. In the sedan I saw the copper faces of officials and, in the rear, women sitting austerely composed. On the running board a man rode with a weapon raised at the sky.

I would begin to construct it even before the tourists put to sea, before the priest returned to the parapet to affirm his belief that my name had not once been spoken. The prisoner had defied water torture and electric shock, his bones had broken around midnight. He had been handed his teeth on fish paper and he had laughed. I constructed the piscators below, the sailors and vendors, growers, shepherds, the informers who would not blanch. The priest confirmed the presence of specialists though I had already constructed them. I observed citizens herded by the laws wearing funereal scarves to cover their faces. A bootblack polished the foot of a specialist when he stepped to the pavement. There was abrupt awkward noise from a radio tuned loudly, then sudden quiet. In the sedan the women sat so tightly together they could have been joined at hips. The priest said coldly, perhaps into the wind, that near dawn Rudy had confessed.

We heard first the coming of the five Morgantas, the sin eaters, who appeared from an alley already deep into their experience. They wore scarves on their heads and their cries sent birds into the air. We followed their broad backs from the fountain to the beach, each woman bow-legged, fat, widowed. We had seen their cheeks running with tears and could only hear now the great sobs they brought forth. The cries echoed in the street. Following them by a few minutes Rudy walked with chains linked between his hands, ankles and neck. But for a cracked leather scapular he was naked. The prisoner rattled in the street, swaying as he walked. His arrival drove attention from the sin eaters who continued their cries but stood uncertain on the beach. Natives backed away from the mechanism erected on the shore.

When the laws gave Rudy to the specialists he spoke and was led to the edge of the water. There he squatted and dropped stools into the sea. The specialists were explaining to him, in calm paternal gestures, the nature of the mechanism. Careful not to step into the water they pointed out various places on the instrument, reassuring him of its efficacy. None of us had ever seen the mechanism before, and when Rudy nodded to the specialists, listening with great care, he relieved our doubts. It seemed that he was asking questions about it, indicating the highest point of it with interest. The specialists were taking their time with the explanation and Rudy finally seemed impressed at the information. At the moment he approached the mechanism Rudy must have known more about its intricacy than anyone present except the specialists. On him the knowledge did not appear desperate.

Seeing Rudy bloodless as an elbow before the wide expanse of sea, I would remember the sandy hue of his skin, the veins in his arms which had given such depth to his muscles. I remembered too that he bit his nails until they bled and would complain that perspiration made his fingers burn. The specialists wore dark suits and neckties, they covered their eves with black glasses; so it was startling to see them lift Rudy b. broken shoulders and place him face down on the mechanism. They had hidden their strength until the last possible moment and though they raised him easily, brought him efficiently into place, their physical labor seemed an embarrassment. It caused their neckties to fly in the breeze, their suits to rumple; the physical process appeared to disturb them too, since it involved a change in demeanor, an acknowledgment of a more overt brutal past.

I could not doubt that Rudy understood. Or that as a yoke contorted his neck, another his pelvis, still another his knees he failed to regret a thing, especially the care and ritual the specialists commanded. When an iron bib was drawn ponderously against his throat he tried to lift his chin to make the act simpler. One of the specialists went down on one knee in front of Rudy's face to explain that because of the yoke on his shoulders any attempt to move would result in severe pain. The same proved to be true at the pelvis and at the knees where the yokes had been placed on opposite sides of his body so that motion on one side caused tension on the other. Then, perhaps, Rudy, like the village, understood not only the principle behind the instrument but its application as well.

In fact and in imagination the mechanism both raised the prisoner in a circular motion—face, pelvis, knees toward the crowd—and exerted three degrees of pressure between yokes and iron bibs. The higher Rudy was lifted the more his bone pried at his skin; the greater the arc of the circle the heavier the pressure became. From my place on the parapet I attempted to see his face as it moved first toward sky, then sea, then sand, and last before the village itself. I wanted to know at what point, if any, Rudy would become unconscious; at which angle, if only one, his jaw would break from his skull. I could not, even in imagination, touch Rudy's perception—his eyes were too fixed, his lips too set, his muscles straining against the inexorable process.

And yet I was certain we would realize at nearly the same instant that by this mechanism the law intended to squeeze crime out of the condemned. The law wished to reveal on the body of the prisoner the evil that moved inside it. To wring brains of their obscure desires, eyes of their dangerous sight. But would Rudy have known it, as I could perceive from a distance and height, when the instrument began to move with greater speed? Or did he only experience the slightly quicker arc as more tension caused by the yokes, each working against the other?

I raised binoculars and looked along the street. Empty, dusty, litter spinning quietly from one end to the other; my village was gathered to a child down at the beach, beyond the palmettos, gathered as if they would greet a ship of explorers laying anchor on our shore by accident, by error. And then I saw a young man on a terrace, leaning in a white shirt open at the chest against a second floor balustrade. His hair greased back, his trousers the color and texture of butter, he smoked a cigarette low between thin fingers. I waited through binoculars for him to turn toward the beach. I did not know his face; he looked foreign but studied the vacant street below with the calm pleasure of familiarity. He began to speak and a woman joined him, a woman who was also pale, untouched by the sun and heat. Wearing a short light dress designed low in the front and back she made me think they were both freshly bathed. I could not help but squeeze my eyes when, after puffing the young man's cigarette, she lifted a breast from her dress and held it for him to kiss. His tongue touched it and I twisted the focus until the couple became the blur of reality during one of our thunder storms. I saw the village then as grains of pure mood, a flux of line, color and motion. I was staring hard at the destruction, my head beginning to ache, fighting against the need to focus.

I must have righted the binoculars too late. As questions and recollection began to form a constellation in my mind the process on the beach stopped. The priest and I exchanged a glance, I saw him swing the fluffy tassel of his cassock cord. Had the instrument broken down? Had Rudy's sentence been commuted? Had someone at last exonerated him? Someone who perhaps could impugn yet another villager?

Rudy was revolving with only the afterimage of the structure's work. I had earlier failed to notice, though I had had weeks to observe closely, that the precipitous slope of his skull made it appear that as a child Rudy had been smacked with a shovel. Now his cheeks were balloons, as if stones filled them. His skin was gray as worm. I could not at last believe that in fact the process was complete, that I had missed the moment of Rudy's death. While the day remained silent, and the natives easily dispersed, I failed to find the young foreign couple anywhere. There was activity on the beach after the body had been removed. I remained in the priest's small chamber. I crippled a tiny chair by sitting in it and coiling my legs around each other. We studied mint tea in porcelain cups, we sniffed the air of the late afternoon. Resplendent light traveled the village from the dim Arab alley to the isolated avenue of the rich where huge palmettos stood stiff and fruity against the sky.

Then only did a deceptive atmosphere enter the chamber, when our priest stood against his fireplace thoughtful as a villain greasing a gun. He tossed the hood of his cassock onto his head and chewed a lip fiercely; it was left to me to adjust my worn necktie and to wipe away the wrinkles in my white linen suit. The looseness of his throat suggested the start of a facial atrophy in our priest; his knuckles against his forehead could only embroider the meaning of the day. We had been drawn by the dust of the crowd to speculate on Rudy's ripe face, on the running pink collars of cheese-colored shirts that the specialists wore. Our priest lifted a feminine hand, gathered thin spirit and concluded it had been grisly for me to warn my wife of death, to incinerate the motorbike and murdered burro and to offer a weak disclaimer of my apprentice and Ponchita, their relationship.

What, citizen, could I resent?

Hadn't Ponchita cried to me to do something? Snuffing a cigarette against the brick of the fireplace she had removed the kettle from the hob and, refusing my help, had lugged it upstairs to our tub.

—Why not fix the plumbing? she had said.

—Fix it so I will not have to heat water in a kettle.

—Do something, my darling. You never really do anything.

As she passed the bedroom door, kettle swaying between her sturdy hips, Ponchita tapped and Rudy replied sharply from inside.

—In a minute, he said.

—Now, my wife answered, while it's still hot.

And in the crawl space below the floor, where the leg of a milking stool had been eaten through and the stool leaned lamely, I worked on my back in the slime. In the water recess below kitchen and upstairs bath a stench of dead rat hung in the air while floating past me toward a drain were shreds of tobacco, fruit pits, tufts of human hair. I felt then the sting of an infected hair on my neck, what had become in the night a festering oozing globe. For the mangled pipes I did what I could with rags, wire and rope. Even then the ground shook beneath me. I quickly lost sight of a shrew that bumped my hand, then saw it watching from a safe distance with its family. When I booted the rotting door and hurried outside as if from a burning auto my leg in the sunlight was greener than a promise. I left muck on the stairs.

Later it would have been impossible to tell our priest, over tea and execution, that I had stood finally peering through the louvers of my own bathroom door: that I saw a body nothing like my own and reflected on the hideousness of such a difference: or that in the steam my wife dipped down to rub herself against him with nipples an inch long and goose flesh on her stomach: or that she stared at his bending penis while I stood caking at the door: how she kneaded his thighs and put a finger to her mouth to quiet the sounds he could not resist, then thrust the same finger between his buttocks. Could I admit that when I experienced the breathlessness of this I thought of death itself? And that, tugging at my Congolese fatigues which bulged all around like clown hats, I recognized the smell as my mother's false teeth? I heard Ponchita praise his sperm count, I saw him violate her face. They had translated the explosion of valuable passion into the calculated self-conscious acts which lovers perform when they are also friends. I would not tell the priest that my wife and her lover had overtaken instinct and had learned to possess experience so that they were loyal to it. The needs of even a child must be met if it is not to be found dead behind a door.

The rest, of course, should only be whispered. Bathers sunning upon tank tracks in the sand: cries of sailors to divers as the engines pump, the winch drips water and scraps of metal are raised from the sea: a blizzard of parachutes dropping high into the mountain: screams of flushing dogs blazing through the woods: the suicide of our priest: bullets promoted in the square, rapes accomplished on the beach: my dog hurtles himself twice, then three times at the door in a gesture of protection. And a new mountain, citizen, cutting the village from the sea, transforming sun into shadow, leaving our promontory a smoking gaseous crater. Washerwomen, picking twigs from linens, pound rock against blood in its monstrous shade. Our whitest wall will corrode, no planting is planned, no harvest. We will not bear olives or pomegranates or figs. There will be no flowers in our smoldering soil. We heard it quaking in the night, a roar of ocean history that toppled verandas and ripped sportscars in the avenue of the rich. We saw burros collapsed on the road, trapped under rock with the bodies of their masters. Specialists are coming to thump our hearts, churn the village bowels: to blast granite and marble: to dig muddy corpses: to raise warplanes and ships from the sea.

Think of me too, citizen, not as whisperer but as what is whispered. At the clutch of dawn I see laws from a lash of the shutter, or shine my torch into the mouth of my chimney to see if it will hide a body large as mine, or listen in a crouch to the foggy voicebox. When the laws begin to roam with Sten guns and the warplanes scream out of the sun the dog sits parallel to me, one ear drooping back to demonstrate the pink vulnerability of his flesh. The she-goat nibbles straw in the parlor, the owls swoop through the villa buffeting walls. My shrew faces me in his armchair. Then at night I strike a match and mine is the only light for miles. Shutters drawn, doors bolted, traps waiting to spring.

Yesterday—I remember transparently, with no obscure edge—I decoded a communiqué borne beneath the legal frequency that caused me to lean toward the window with sovereignty and vision. I removed my felony shoes clotted with mud, breathed deeply the mist on the veranda and surveyed the rumbling coast through binoculars. I held Mother's teeth in my palm. It was there before the travelers and laws, in every murder of the messenger, in each mapmaker's compass, in the slime and the mortar of the first wall, the whitest wall of the village. Putting myself at rest until the moon gleamed like a wounded lion's eye I stalked toward the village.

My first was a native face, exotic and limp, napping on his father's patio. There was light at the back of the house, a dull bulb where women spoke softly of something serious. I scooped the dark bundle and dropped it into my fruit basket among bananas and cool limes. A child of lustrous sexless eyes, lips poised in bewilderment, an intoxicating face. I set it on a pillow in the villa and ordered the dog to keep it in place. That was evening.

I watched toys fly from a crater on the beach, saw baby prints, the leaf of a dwarfish hand feel for a tiny shovel and drag it into the pit. Sand flew to my feet. The child sat in a life preserver of rubber, clutching a duck's feathered head. He stared at me as I lifted him, struck my head with the heart of his shovel, but not once did he cry out. I nestled in the armchair with the radio tuned, holding in each arm a child. They slept peacefully and hotly against my bare chest. I would take the child of a traveler next, and the child would be a girl. I studied their useless feet, their bodies feeling stuffed with down and light as muffins. I cut lemons into the shape of sailors and moved my fingers like a rabbit's ears. Together we jammed figs in our teeth to bite the ancient gummy fruit. The next I would take as she slept in an auto the color of mercury. I would take her without disturbing the cookie in her hand. It was the warm time of day noted by all who pass here for its exquisite quiet and solace. The child would have parrot green eyes.

Then it will, I suppose, be dawn when ships enter the harbor. In fog at dawn the slow steady hum of engines and the perceptible slicing of the waves. Ships with foreign flags baying in the wind will enter dimly to elevate their vast metal guns at our village and mountainside. And I will watch from the stone tower as an army examines the wreckage of our fountain where crabs have come to nest in the shallow mud. The vessels can float to sea and back, can ring a hundred bells while we wait for the disembarkation.

Now we redden and ache, Ponchita and I, ignoring the deliberate rhythm of dying, awaiting the sudden sunburst into myth. We crush teeth against teeth. We are, in a sense, still lovers.